Home for Meow

Two Fur One

Home for Meow

Two Fur One

Reese Eschmann

Scholastic Inc.

Library of Congress Cataloging-in-Publication Data available

ISBN 978-1-338-78401-5

10 9 8 7 6 5 4 3 2 1 23 24 25 26 27

Printed in the U.S.A. 40

First edition, February 2023

Book design by Stephanie Yang

Table of Contents

1

The World's Longest Cat

"Welcome to The Purrfect Cup, the best and only cat café in town! Can I interest you in a cap-*purr*-ccino?"

The customer standing in front of me looks confused and nervous. Probably because our family's cat, Pepper, is sitting on the counter staring at him. Her tail is perfectly still and her eyes don't blink. Pepper lifts her paw and licks her claws slowly, never taking her eyes off the customer.

"Um, can I just get a cup of water?" he asks.

"Sure, I guess," I say. "But if you change your mind, we also have hot chocolate with marsh-*meow*-lows. Or I could make you some *purr*-itos and avo-*cat*-o toast."

"Kira Parker," Mama says sternly. "What are you going on about?"

Mama finishes wiping down one of the tables in the café and joins me behind the register. She pours a cup of water for the customer. "Sorry about that. We're actually all out of our homemade marshmallows. And we've never served burritos or avocado toast," she says. Then she turns to me.

"Kira, why don't you go help your father in the kitchen?"

"I *was* helping him, but he sent me back out here because I put too many chocolate chips in the cookie dough." He also said I put too many chocolate chips in my mouth, but Mama doesn't need to know that.

"Well, go ask him if you can help again. And take it *slow* this time."

I don't know if I *can* take it slow. I feel as restless as a kitten who hasn't learned the difference between day and night, and stays up all night pouncing on your toes. We haven't had school in *three* days! Our principal closed the school so our teachers could listen to some people talk about how to teach. I thought they already knew! I'm not sure what more there is to learn. Teaching kids is probably way easier than taking care of cats, which is what I've been doing all week.

I love hanging out with the cats that live in our family's cat café, The Purrfect Cup. It's the most wonderful and cozy place in the world. The cats stay here with us until we can find them the perfect fur-ever homes. They climb on the shelves lining the walls and play with all the toys we leave around the café. Usually the cats love watching the customers and walking up to them to ask

for belly rubs. But today, even the cats seem bored!

They're lying on top of tables and chairs with their legs all the way stretched out, like they're trying to take up as much space as they can. I see a cat lie down on top of a customer's laptop and refuse to move. Another one dips its paw in a customer's glass of iced tea. I think it must be about to rain or something. My best human friend, Alex Patel, told me that cats can tell when it's about to rain, and they also get restless. It's too bad Alex isn't around to tell me more cool facts. She and her mom went on vacation while school's closed.

I turn to my best nonhuman friend, Pepper. She stops licking her paw when she sees me looking at her.

"Want to go back to the kitchen?" I ask. In response, she rolls over onto her back and sticks her legs straight up in the air. I think she's tired of going back and forth between the kitchen and the café too.

My brain is usually full of *great ideas* for things to do when I don't have school. Sometimes I even have *great ideas* when I'm at school, which gets me into trouble, like that time I decided the school library needed more books about cats, so I wrote my own. I probably shouldn't have thrown the other books away, but I needed space for mine! Right now, I can't think of any *great ideas*! My brain is as empty as the library shelves after my teacher took my cat books down.

Pepper follows me into the kitchen behind the café, where Dad is making coffee cake for the afternoon crowd of customers. His coffee cake is perfectly buttery and cinnamony, and it has a layer of brown sugar streusel that's as thick as the cake. Just how I like it.

"Hey, Dad," I say. "Mama sent me back here to

help you. Is there anything I can do? I'll be more careful this time."

"Can you hand me that bag of powdered sugar? You can help me sprinkle it on the coffee cake if you go real slow."

"Sure!" I say. I run over to grab the bag of powdered sugar and—*whoops*. I didn't know it was already open. I pick it up by the bottom, and all the powdered sugar dumps out onto me, Pepper, and the floor.

Dad sighs.

"Yeah," I say. "I'll go check on the cats."

I walk back out to the café. Mama's talking to a woman near the front of the café. The woman doesn't seem to be a customer because she's not ordering anything. She is wearing a huge belt that's holding all kinds of tools. Hammers, a measuring tape, and screwdrivers. I wonder what she and Mama are talking about.

My little brother, Ryan, is sitting at a table near the café door, right by Mama. I plop down into a chair next to him so I can listen to Mama's conversation.

Ryan is watching a show on Mama's iPad. He offers me an earbud. "I don't know why you don't want to sit and watch TV," he says. "I'm having the best day ever!"

"You know I'm bad at sitting," I say. "My blood's as hot as a donut coming out of the fryer!"

"Remember that time you burned your finger

on the fryer and made that funny noise?" Ryan laughs. "Maybe *that* was the best day ever."

I scowl at him. "Shh! I'm trying to hear what Mama's saying to that lady. Do you know who she is?"

Ryan shrugs. "She looks important. Maybe she's going to use that hammer to finally hang a giant picture of me on the wall. That would really brighten this place up!"

"The Purrfect Cup doesn't need any brightening up. It's already perfect! Plus, your face would scare all the customers away—oh no, look, your face scared the lady away already!"

Mama and the woman move away from us. They walk around The Purrfect Cup. The woman holds her measuring tape up to the walls and the cats and the cats on the walls, then takes notes on a little pad of paper.

"What is she doing?" I whisper. "Why does she want to know how long our cats are?"

"Maybe Mama is entering us into the World's Longest Cat contest," Ryan says. "That'd be awesome!"

I get up to ask the woman what she's doing, but she turns to Mama and shakes her hand. A bunch of cards fall out of one of the pockets on her belt and land on the floor. I pick them up.

"I'll send this quote right over," the woman says. "And unless any urgent jobs come up, I should be able to stop by tomorrow. Looking forward to it."

"Thanks so much, Mrs. Talbot," Mama says. "We'll see you soon!"

I hold up the fallen cards, but the woman is very tall—so tall, she doesn't notice me when she walks out the door. I look down at the cards. They have her name and phone number on them.

AMY TALBOT
CONTRACTOR | PLUMBER | GENERAL DO-GOODER
(800) 555-0100

"Why are we going to see that lady soon?" I ask Mama. "Is she from the World's Longest Cat contest?"

"No." Mama laughs. "She's a contractor who just moved to town. She fixes up houses and shops and makes them better."

"That sounds like a fun job," I say. "But what's that got to do with us?"

"Dad and I are hiring her to do some work in The Purrfect Cup. We're going to tear down a wall to make the café space bigger and get Dad a new oven for the kitchen."

My stomach does a twist and turn. I feel like I just ate a whole pile of *purr*-itos and now I'm going to be sick.

"But The Purrfect Cup is already perfect!" I protest. "It's in the name! Why would we change it? You'll upset the cats. This is their home."

It's not just the cats that'll be upset. I love The Purrfect Cup just the way it is. It's my favorite place in the whole, wide world. I don't want anything about it to change. I feel desperate.

"What if we just hang up a picture of Ryan to brighten up the place?" I ask. "Then we wouldn't have to tear down a whole wall—"

"Kira," Mama says softly. "I know change is hard. But this is a good thing. Our space needs to grow just like our business has. We'll even have more room for all your ideas!"

"There's already the perfect amount of room for ideas! Mama, look at Pepper! She's getting so upset."

Pepper rolls over onto her back and plays dead.

"We're doing this for Pepper and all the cats." Mama sighs, giving Pepper an exasperated smile. "Haven't you noticed how restless they've been? In the new, bigger café, they'll have more room to play and run around."

"They're only restless because it's about to rain," I grumble, but then I look outside and see the sun shining bright. "Sometime this week, it'll rain for sure. And what if the cats don't like all the noise that Mrs. Talbot makes when she's hammering stuff?"

"Don't worry, Kira, we're going to keep the cats safe during the construction. We'll close the café for a few weeks while Mrs. Talbot is working. Our family will take all the cats to your cousin's house, and we'll stay there until the café is ready."

Oh no. This is even worse than I thought! It's like taking a bite of broccoli only to discover that it's stuffed with peas. The broccoli was bad enough! I don't want to be away from the café for weeks. My cousins live *so* far away—almost two whole hours. I like them because they have lots of animals and their cats roam free, watching over the cows and chickens that live in their barn. But our cats hate leaving home. I'm not sure they would like a barn.

"We can't close the café!" I say. "Where will people get their coffee and cat pies?"

"They'll have to make their own coffee for a little while," Mama says. "I'm sorry, Kira, but this is what's best for our family, our business, and our home. I hope you'll understand when it's all finished."

I understand one thing.

I'm going to need a really *great idea* if I'm going to stop Mrs. Talbot from tearing down The Purrfect Cup tomorrow.

2

Cat Count

When I'm feeling upset, there's one thing I can always count on to help me relax and feel better: making art!

"I'm going to Mr. Anderson's to get art supplies," I tell Mama.

She looks relieved. "I'm glad. I'm sure that will

help. You can even draw some ideas for the new space! Bring Mr. Anderson some apple pie bars. And take Pepper with you. She's been just as bored as you these past few days!"

Pepper and I walk to Mr. Anderson's craft shop, Anderson's Artsy Abode. It's not a far walk, because Mr. Anderson's shop is next door to The Purrfect Cup! I wonder if Mama remembers that his wall is right next to ours. Mrs. Talbot might knock it down when she tries to make more space in the café!

Inside, Anderson's Artsy Abode is bright and colorful. It's filled with shelves of paint, markers, and fancy paper. It feels just as perfect and cozy as The Purrfect Cup.

Pepper meows when she sees Mr. Anderson.

"I think she's saying hello," I say. "I'm also saying hello! And Mama says hello too."

Mr. Anderson is standing by the register. I set the apple pie bars on the counter in front of him.

"Hello to you too, Kira and Pepper!" Mr. Anderson says. His voice is always friendly and warm. He's one of my favorite customers. "No school today, right? That must be fun!"

"Not really," I say. "Someone was in the café measuring our cats and talking about tearing down The Purrfect Cup. And I haven't had any *great ideas* all day."

"I'm sorry you're feeling upset, Kira,"

Mr. Anderson says. "I heard about the renovations."

"Are you worried they might tear down your wall too?"

Mr. Anderson chuckles. "Not at all! There's a big closet space between the café wall and my shop. It's been empty for years. I'm glad your parents are finally going to put it to good use."

I didn't know about the empty space. But it doesn't change the fact that Mama and Dad are trying to improve the café, even though it's already perfect! I wouldn't dye Pepper's perfect gray-and-white fur purple. I mean, I did try one time, but I learned my lesson. She looked terrible.

"You know," Mr. Anderson continues, "this place could use some sprucing up too. I've been thinking about hiring a contractor to build some new shelves."

I look down at my hand and realize that I'm still holding Mrs. Talbot's business cards.

I get the start of an idea. It's not a full idea yet—it wouldn't win the World's Longest Cat contest—but it's at least the size of a kitten. And I'm sure it will grow.

Mama told Mrs. Talbot to come tear down The Purrfect Cup tomorrow. But Mrs. Talbot said she could only come if she doesn't have any *urgent* jobs, and Mr. Anderson seems like he really needs new shelves. If Mrs. Talbot is busy helping him, she won't have any time to come work on the café. That would give me a few extra days to convince Mama and Dad that changing The Purrfect Cup is as bad an idea as that time I sold cat food in the café and made the whole place smell like fish.

"Why don't you take one of Mrs. Talbot's cards?" I ask Mr. Anderson. "I bet she could build your shelves. You should probably ask her to build them *right away*!"

"Thanks, Kira," Mr. Anderson says, taking one of Mrs. Talbot's cards. "It is pretty urgent. We just got a huge shipment of new art supplies in—and we have nowhere to put them! That reminds me, I was hoping you'd test these new paint pens for me. They look like a marker, but they have a paintbrush on the end. Want to try them out?"

"Yes, please!" I say. "Coloring and painting always help my brain relax so I can have more ideas. Now I can color and paint at the same time!"

Pepper gives the paint pens a lick of approval.

"Take a few of those big sheets of paper with you," Mr. Anderson says, pointing to one of his shelves.

The paper is on the other side of the store. I walk over to grab it, passing the big window at the front of the shop. As I do, I catch a glimpse of something walking by outside.

"Mr. Anderson, did you see that?" I say. "That looked like a fluffy tail to me!"

The hairs on Pepper's back stand up. She must have seen it too! I turn to Mr. Anderson, but he looks confused. "Sorry, Kira, I didn't see anything."

"It looked like a cat's tail," I say. "Oh no. I think one of the cats got away from The Purrfect Cup!"

I run outside, but I don't see any sign of the cat

with the fluffy tail. Pepper and I burst through the door of The Purrfect Cup.

"What's wrong, Kira?" Mama asks. "You look worried. Still upset about Mrs. Talbot?"

"No, it's not that. Well, it is, but it's not *just* that! I saw a cat walk by Mr. Anderson's. I think one of our cats got away!"

Mama's hands fly to her chest. "There have been a lot of customers coming in and out. I sure hope a cat didn't slip by unnoticed."

"We need to do a cat count!" Ryan says, standing up.

"Mama, how many cats are living at The Purrfect Cup right now?"

She looks over some papers on her desk. "It

looks like . . . fourteen. Not including Pepper."

"Okay. One . . . two . . . three . . ." I walk around the room, counting every cat in the café. My heart beats fast. They're all so cute, with perfect whiskers and perfect squishy faces. They're my best friends. I really hope one of them didn't get lost outside. This is exactly why we can't leave the café. The cats aren't safe when they're not in The Purrfect Cup!

I keep counting. "Twelve . . . thirteen . . . fourteen . . . FIFTEEN?"

I gasp. The fluffy-tailed cat wasn't running *away* from The Purrfect Cup. It was sneaking in!

3

The Odd Couple

"Fifteen?" Mama exclaims. "That can't be right. Are you sure you didn't count Pepper?"

"I'm positive!" I say.

"Which cat is the new one?" Ryan asks. "I can't tell!"

"It has a really fluffy brown-and-black tail," I say.

Mama, Ryan, and I walk around the café, looking closely at each of the cats. They stare at us suspiciously, like they think *we're* the weird ones! But we didn't sneak into a cat café. Pepper walks alongside me, sniffing all the cats. I wonder if she's trying to see which one doesn't smell familiar.

"I don't see a fluffy brown tail," Mama says. "Are you sure that's what it looked like? If we can't find it, we'll have to take all of them to the vet! Dr. Delgado will be able to tell which one snuck in."

"I'm sure it had a huge brown tail," I say. "With some black markings . . ."

"That one has black markings," Ryan says. He points to a cat sitting on top of a basket. It's a white cat with brown-and-black markings along its face and back. It's staring at the wall—and sitting on its tail!

I can see the cat's fluffy tail sticking out from beneath it. It's sitting on a brown-and-white-spotted blanket in the basket. I run over to the new cat. "We found you! You're really good at hiding," I say. "That was pretty smart to sit on your tail so I wouldn't recognize you."

The cat is one of the biggest I've ever seen. If there really is a World's Longest Cat contest, it would totally win! I look into its big, light brown eyes. It looks kind—and a little bit scared.

"It's okay," I whisper. "You came to the right place."

"We're going to take care of you," Ryan says. "Aren't we, Mama?"

Before Mama can answer, the cat's body moves up and down like it's floating on a boat in the middle of a storm. But it isn't moving any of its legs! The movement is coming from the blanket in the basket.

"Uh, why is that blanket under the cat moving?" Ryan asks.

I gasp. "That's not a blanket . . . it's fur!"

Just then, a dog's head pops up out of the basket! It's a small dog with big, floppy brown ears, and a black-and-white body. Its huge eyes look up

at me. They're so cute and sad. All I want to do is give the dog a hug.

"Awww," I say before I can help myself. I never understood the meaning of *puppy eyes* until now. I've always thought that dogs were slobbery and stinky, and nowhere near as cute and smart as cats. But this dog actually smells good, and he was smart enough to hide beneath the fluffy-tailed cat.

My heart swells inside my chest. Sometimes I think I have two hearts. One is filled with love for my favorite humans, like my family and Alex and Mr. Anderson. The other one holds all my love for Pepper and the other cats at the café. But now I feel like I might have a *third* heart. I may not know this dog very well yet, but I sure love him.

The dog whines softly. I wonder if he feels guilty for hiding. "You're such a sweet puppy. Don't feel bad. It's okay."

I reach my hand out to see if the dog wants to sniff me, but the cat with the fluffy tail hisses! It moves to stand between me and the dog.

I look at Mama for help. "I think she must be

protecting the dog," Mama says. "Goodness, they're an odd couple, aren't they? We always get animals from the shelter. But they've never just shown up at the café before! What are we going to do?"

Dad comes out from the kitchen. "What's going on out here?"

When he sees the dog, his eyebrows shoot up so far that they make his forehead get all wrinkly. "I knew I should have stayed in the kitchen," he says.

I feel like I'm in the kitchen right now, because my brain is cooking up another *great idea.* The Purrfect Cup has never had a dog before, but there's a first time for everything! Dogs don't purr, it's true, but I'm sure they like cups. Everybody likes cups. And that means this dog belongs at The Purrfect Cup as much as the new cat does. They'll need some time to get used to living here, which means we can't close the café for Mrs. Talbot!

When I have a *great idea*, Dad likes to say I'm a pretty smart cookie. I don't really know what that means. I didn't think cookies had brains. But they do know how to be delicious and sweet, which I guess means they're smart! And I think this dog and cat are smart cookies for wandering into The Purrfect Cup. They knew we'd take care of them!

"I think we should keep them both," I say. My

voice is loud and confident. "Wouldn't that be a *great idea*? And look, Mama, they're already so cozy in that basket. They don't need any more space. The Purrfect Cup is the perfect size for them. I know you think we should shake things up at the café. But what's better at shaking than a dog? Look, he's shaking his tail now!"

The dog's ears perk up as I speak, and his tail thumps against the sides of the basket.

"It's called *wagging* a tail, not shaking," Ryan says, rolling his eyes. "Don't you know anything about dogs?"

"Nope!" I say. "But I'm ready to learn."

"Okay, okay, slow down," Mama says. "I'm not so sure that having a dog in the café is a good idea.

We don't want to stress out the other cats. And we're already going to have to pack everyone up to leave soon before renovations start."

"But, Mama," I say, "you said the cats have been restless. Maybe it's not because they need us to tear down a wall. Maybe they just need someone new to play with! Look, none of them seem bored now."

In fact, the cats are on high alert. Every single cat in the café is staring at the newcomers. Pepper is frozen by my side. I think she's hoping that if she doesn't move, the dog won't notice her. But he's such a sweet puppy, he doesn't even try to bother any of the cats. He stays by his fluffy-tailed friend.

"I'm not so sure the cats want to play," Mama says again. "They might be scared."

Dad holds up his hand as I open my mouth to protest. "We're not making a final decision about either of these animals right now. First we need to make sure they're fed and healthy."

Mama nods in agreement. Dad makes some plain chicken and rice for the dog, and puts out a bowl of cat food for the new cat. We set the food bowls a few feet apart, but the dog and cat refuse to eat until we move the bowls close together. Both of their tails swish happily as they eat, and they don't mind at all that they keep bumping into each other! Then, they drink water out of the same bowl. After that, their eyes don't look so sad and scared anymore. They climb back into the basket and snuggle in together. The dog rests his head on the side of the basket and blinks slowly. I think he's falling asleep!

"Mama, look how happy he is here!" I say. "He thinks the café is *purrfect*. Or *paw*-fect. Or *slobber*-some."

"*Slobber*-some?" Ryan raises an eyebrow at me.

"You know, like awesome, but for dogs because they love slobber."

Ryan rolls his eyes. "You really don't know anything about dogs."

I ignore him and turn back to Mama. "Are you sure we can't let him stay? I bet our customers would love a dog as much as they love the cats!

We might even be able to find him an adoptive home."

Mama sighs. "Let's take this one step at a time," she reminds me. "Now that they're fed, the next step is to take them to the vet and see if they're healthy. Why don't you go with your dad to see Dr. Delgado?"

I'm not sure how I feel about taking things *one step at a time*. When Granny came to stay with us and I had to help run the café, she told me about taking things one step at a time, just like you do when you're following a recipe.

But The Purrfect Cup doesn't have time to take things slow right now. There's nothing wrong with getting the zoomies and running around.

Our cats do it all the time. I have to move fast if I'm going to find a home for the odd couple *and* stop Mrs. Talbot from tearing down the café. But then Dad tells me to go upstairs to find the leash I bought for Pepper last year so we can put it on the dog. Pepper did *not* like wearing a leash. That wasn't one of my *great ideas*. But I'm sure that this is.

Even if I have to take it slow.

4

Mysteries and Microchips

On the way to see Dr. Delgado at the animal hospital, Dad and I try to come up with names for the new cat and dog.

"Well, the new dog is a beagle, so how about we call him, uh . . . Beagle Man?"

I smack my palm against my forehead. "We

can't call him Beagle Man! Names are supposed to be cute and fun, and Beagle Man sounds like he's trying to be a superhero! He likes to hide in baskets, not fight crime."

"Well, then, how about Spot?" Dad asks. "That's a good name for a dog."

The beagle *does* have a lot of spots. He looks up at Dad and pants happily. "Okay," I say. "I like Spot. And we'll call the cat Swish, because her big tail is so swishy, and that's how I found her."

In response, Dad peers down into the cat carrier where Swish is sitting. She didn't like being separated from Spot, but at least she can see him from the front of the carrier. And she looks pretty comfortable now. When she first got in the carrier, she seemed scared, but then she found the cat treats and soft blankets I'd put in there for her, and she settled down.

"Hey, little Swishy-Swish," Dad says. "How you doin' in there?"

"Don't worry," I tell her. "We're almost to the vet! Then you and Spot can sit next to each other again."

I use the time alone with Dad to find out how he *really* feels about Mrs. Talbot coming to tear down the café.

"She's not going to tear the whole place down!" He laughs. "Just one wall. And I am looking forward to a new oven. But I know how you feel, Kira. My pops, your grandfather, was in the military when I was your age, so we had to move around a lot. It was really hard going from place to place. Sometimes I thought I'd rather live in one old house with peeling paint and crumbling walls than have to pack up my stuff *again*. But then I learned that a home is more than paint and walls."

Before I can ask Dad what he means, we arrive at the animal hospital. Dr. Delgado looks surprised to see us with a dog! I don't blame him. Everyone in town knows we're cat people. But Spot is pretty cute. And not too slobbery. I still feel like I have three hearts when I look at him. And I think he loves Swish with all his hearts. When we set her cat carrier down in Dr. Delgado's exam room, Spot runs over to push his nose up against the door.

"So, Parkers," Dr. Delgado says. "I see you have a new, uh, addition to the family?"

"Well, let's not get ahead of ourselves," Dad says, but then he scratches Spot behind his ears. "These two wandered into The Purrfect Cup today. We're calling them Spot and Swish. We were hoping you could look them over. Make sure it's safe for them to be around the other cats until we figure out what to do."

Dr. Delgado takes Swish out of the cat carrier. He takes turns peering into Spot's and Swish's ears and mouths. He checks the spaces between their toes and listens to their hearts. The whole time, they stand so close to each other that their front paws touch.

"Well, they're both healthy," Dr. Delgado says. "Someone has definitely been feeding them and giving them water. They even smell like they just got a bath!"

"Does that mean they have a family somewhere?" I ask. All three of my hearts feel heavy and sad when I think that Spot and Swish might be far away from their home. They probably feel how I feel when I try to picture The Purrfect Cup looking different from how it looks now—lost and confused.

"I don't know," Dr. Delgado says thoughtfully. He scratches his chin while he thinks. "Some animals, like all the cats in your café, have microchips. That helps their owners or the shelters find them if they get lost. Spot and Swish don't have microchips or collars."

"Hm, that's interesting," says Dad. "I wonder who's been feeding them."

"Could be someone doing a good deed," Dr. Delgado says. "But I'll ask my assistant to check all the websites that we use to help locate lost pets. We might find out that they have a home! But one thing's for sure."

"What's that?" I ask.

"Wherever these two came from, they came together. They've really bonded! And people say cats and dogs can't get along." Dr. Delgado laughs.

"See?" I say to Dad. "Dr. Delgado thinks it's silly to say that cats and dogs won't get along."

"We'll take them back to the café," Dad says. "But then we're calling the animal shelter. They can take care of Spot while we find out where these two came from."

Oh no. I feel so worried, and all I want to do is pull Spot and Swish in for an extra-tight hug. Dr. Delgado said that Spot and Swish were *bonded*. I can't let Spot go to the animal shelter.

"The animal shelter is closed," Dr. Delgado says. Spot's ears perk up, and so do mine. "The owner, Peter, is driving a few states over to help rescue some goats. There's someone there looking after the animals, but they can't take any new ones right now. Don't worry, though, I think Peter will be back tomorrow. I'll call you if my assistant finds anything."

I scratch my chin, just like Dr. Delgado did when he was thinking. Maybe that's a trick adults know to help their brains work better. I wonder if there's a hair at the bottom of my chin that reaches all the way into my brain and tells it to wake up because there's a mystery that needs solving! Spot and Swish are healthy and clean. That means someone's been giving them food and water. We just don't know who. I'm *sure* they have a home out there, somewhere. And no one should be separated from their home. This feels like a recipe that's missing a page of instructions.

If I can find the missing ingredients and figure out where Spot and Swish came from, then they won't have to be separated!

I have to solve this mystery before the animal shelter reopens, and I still need to make sure that Mrs. Talbot is too busy to come to The Purrfect Cup. And I have to do it all by tomorrow.

I sure hope my *great ideas* grow big enough to win the World's Longest Cat contest, because this isn't going to be easy.

5

Spiders and Sisters

Spot and Swish spend the night upstairs in our apartment. They seem right at home on the couch in the living room. Ryan and I sit next to them and watch a movie. Pepper spends the *whole* movie standing next to the TV stand, staring at Spot. Every few minutes, Spot looks up at her and his tail does a hopeful little wag. Pepper responds by turning her head away and pretending she isn't looking at him. Then he goes back to snoozing next to Swish.

As soon as the movie ends, Pepper seems to make up her mind about Spot. I hold my breath while she crosses the room. I don't know what she's about to do! Then she hops up onto the couch and curls into a ball on the other side of Spot. Swish gets up and starts licking the tops of both their heads. Ryan and I look at each other and smile.

"Maybe Mama and Dad will let them stay," Ryan says. "Spot and Swish are couch people. Just like us."

"I don't know. Mama and Dad seemed to have their minds made up about sending Spot to the shelter. Just like they made up their minds about tearing down The Purrfect Cup."

Ryan frowns. He doesn't like the idea of The Purrfect Cup changing, either. Especially after he asked to paint the new wall blue and Mama said she'd already decided on lime green.

I try to cheer him up. "But I bet Spot and Swish have a home with a super cozy couch somewhere! Their family probably misses them so much. Tomorrow, I'll remind Mr. Anderson how *urgently* he needs new shelves, then I'll find Spot and Swish's home before the animal shelter opens."

"Do you have any clues about where they came from?" Ryan asks.

I shake my head. Ryan sighs.

"How are you going to solve a mystery with no clues?"

"I'll get a clue tomorrow!"

"Clues don't show just up at your front door, Kira."

Just then, the buzzer in our apartment goes off. That means someone is downstairs. Spot sits up straight and lets out a long, low howl when he hears the buzzer. Dad comes out from his bedroom.

"Pizza's here!"

"Yes!" Ryan and I shout together. We love when

Dad orders pizza from Pizza My Heart, the best pizza shop in town. All their pizzas come shaped like a heart. Spot sniffs the air, then runs downstairs to greet the pizza delivery person. I follow him downstairs. His tail wags excitedly as Dad opens the door, but I'm not sure whether he's excited for the food or the pizza man!

The pizza man smiles wide when he sees Spot and Swish. I think he recognizes them.

"Hey there, Pepperoni and Sausage," he says. "What are you two doing here?"

"You know Spot and Swish!" I say excitedly. "Are you their family?"

"No, but they come by the pizza shop all the time. My boss gives them food and water. They especially love her homemade pepperoni and sausage."

"Oh," I say. I feel disappointed. "I was hoping you knew who they belonged to. We're trying to find their home."

"You should come by Pizza My Heart tomorrow and talk to my boss. She's the one who feeds them. She might know where they're from. But when you come, wear some rain boots. We have a leaky pipe and the floor has been a bit soggy. Unlike our pizza crust, which is still nice and crisp."

He hands Dad the pizza and a business card from their shop. Seeing the business card makes the *great idea* I had in Mr. Anderson's shop grow. I bet Mrs. Talbot could fix their soggy floor problem! That sounds way more urgent than fixing the wall at The Purrfect Cup. Mrs. Talbot will have to help them right away. When the pizza man leaves, I turn to Ryan and smile.

"Turns out clues *do* show up at the front door."

"Whatever." Ryan shrugs. He turns to Dad. "Can I give Spot and Swish all my pepperoni and sausage?"

♥🐾♥

The next morning, Pepper and I sit at one of the tables in The Purrfect Cup.

"What time is Mrs. Talbot coming?" I ask Mama.

"Not until later," she says. "I think she's stopping by Mr. Anderson's first."

I keep my face still, but inside I feel like a kitten swimming in a pool of cat treats. My idea is working! But I need to find a way to get even more time. Mr. Anderson's shelves won't take that long.

I look at the wall that Mrs. Talbot wants to tear down. A cat jumps on one shelf with a loose nail, and it wobbles beneath the cat's paws. There are three other cats trying to squeeze into a box on the floor, right in front of the spot where I colored on the wall in crayon when I was five. That was one of my first *great ideas.* Dad tried to paint over it, but I can still see the cat-shaped scribbles underneath. I love this wall so much. I don't want it to change.

Spot and Swish are sitting under the table by my feet. I remind myself that we're getting ready for an adventure. I'm going to take Spot and Swish to the pizza shop to see if someone there knows how to find their home. But first, I need my adventure supplies. I found Ryan's old baby stroller in the closet between the café wall and Mr. Anderson's shop. Pepper and Swish will love sitting in the stroller while we walk to Pizza My Heart. There was a lot of cool stuff in the closet! I didn't even know it existed, but now I want it to stay forever. I even found a cane that Granny left when she was visiting, which is perfect because all adventurers need walking sticks! And I packed a few pairs of hats and gloves just in case it gets cold.

"I didn't know cat cafés had dogs!" I look up to see a girl about my age smiling at Spot. He starts to wag his tail super fast! He's been doing this all morning whenever he thinks one of the cats wants to be his friend. Sometimes a cat comes up to him, and his whole body shakes while he tries to sit super still so he doesn't scare them. Most of the time the cats run away before they get too close, and Spot whimpers. But then Swish cuddles in close and he seems to feel better!

When Spot sees the girl looking at him, his tail thumps so hard against the ground that it sounds like a drum.

"We don't usually have dogs at the café," I say. "This is our first one!"

"Cool! You should get some spiders next," the girl says. "I wish more people knew that they make really good pets."

"Uh, good idea!" I say, even though I'm not so sure. Spiders may not have any slobber or fur that gets everywhere, but they're kind of creepy. Plus, Pepper chases spiders around the house—and sometimes she eats them. I don't think Mama and Dad would want the café to be full of pets that the cats will eat.

"Aww, I like that cat's huge tail," says another girl who looks a little older than me. She walks over to join us. "The dog is using it as a pillow!"

"They're best friends, and they love to snuggle," I say. "Mama calls them an *odd couple*. She calls me Kira, which is my name, by the way."

"I'm Abbey Jacobson," says the first girl. "This is Darby Jacobson. We're kind of sisters."

I raise an eyebrow. I didn't know it was possible to *kind of* have a sister. As far as I know, I'm fully stuck with Ryan for the rest of my life.

Darby sees the confused look on my face. "She means we're stepsisters. My dad married her mom, and now we all live in a house together."

Abbey scowls. "I don't like saying *stepsister*. It's weird! Stepsisters in books are always evil."

The two girls stare at each other, like they're trying to figure out which one of them is the evil one. Darby shrugs and looks back at me. "Abbey's mom really wants us to get cats that are sisters. She says it'll help us bond, since we don't have anything in common. Abbey loves bugs and I think they're gross! I prefer birds because they're so dainty and cute."

"Birds are too colorful! Who wants a bright yellow pet? Plus, they eat spiders. So rude."

"You know what else is rude?" Darby counters. "Not making your bed. I like to keep our room clean, but Abbey thinks laundry is a waste of time."

Abbey nods seriously. "It *is*."

Darby sighs. "See. We have nothing in common! But Abbey's mom still thinks we should get two cats and name them after famous sisters. Like Anna and Elsa."

"Or Charlotte and Emily," says Abbey. "I don't even know who they are! They wrote super old books or something."

"Or Beyoncé and Solange," Darby says. "I'm not going to name my cat Beyoncé! Even if my cat is a queen, she'd never be *the* queen, you know?"

Both girls sigh. I think they might have more

in common than they think. They both hate famous sisters.

I clear my throat. "Well, if you want to adopt cats, you've come to the right place! Let me ask my mom if we have two girl cats from the same litter. That would make them sisters! And while you're here, I would really appreciate it if you would tell my mom how much you love this wall."

Abbey raises an eyebrow at the wobbly shelf.

I find Mama at the back of the café talking to Darby and Abbey's parents, the Jacobsons. She tells me to show Darby and Abbey a pair of tabby cats that are sisters.

Both girls frown when they see them. I'm not

so sure how I feel about that. The cats are perfectly cute!

"They're *orange*," Darby says. "And we have hot pink walls in our bedroom. Don't you think those colors would clash?"

"I'd prefer a black cat," says Abbey. "Maybe one that had eight legs. And was a spider."

"Well, maybe you'll change your mind after you play with them a bit!" I say. "Cats have a way of winning you over. I have to go on my adventure now, though. But if you're still here when I get back, we can play with the cats!"

Both girls' heads turn around to stare at me when I say the word *adventure*.

"What kind of adventure are you going on?"

Abbey asks. "Are you going to make a list of all the different kinds of bugs in town? We can compare."

"Are you going to *squash* all the bugs in town?" Darby retorts. "Because I'd be down for that."

Abbey tucks her thumbs into her palm and stretches out her other eight fingers so that they look like creepy, crawly spider legs. She inches them toward Darby's face.

I talk loudly, hoping that'll get them to stop acting so weird. "Actually, I'm going to Pizza My Heart to see if the pizza boss knows where Spot and Swish came from."

"Ooh, I love their heart-shaped pizzas!" Darby says.

"Can we come?" asks Abbey. "Last time I went to Pizza My Heart there were cobwebs in the corners. I bet they have tons of spiders."

"Sure!" I say. "Adventures are always better with more people. And I might need help finding clues."

I ask Mama and the Jacobsons if Abbey and Darby can come with me, and they say yes. Mama looks relieved that I'm not asking her any more questions about the café wall, but as we leave I tuck Mrs. Talbot's business cards into my pocket. Darby and Abbey help me put Pepper's old leash on Spot. Then we set Pepper and Swish in the baby stroller and pull down the mesh cover so they stay safe inside.

"They look way cuter in there than my little brother, Ryan, ever did!" I say. "I remember when Mama brought him home and he had this squishy, wrinkly face. I guess it was kind of cute. I wish I had a sister too!"

"Don't be so sure," Darby says out of the corner of her mouth. "We fight all the time."

"Well, yeah, of course. Ryan and I fight too. And we make a LOT of faces at each other."

"Really? But I thought siblings were supposed to get along?" Abbey asks.

"I mean, I don't want to get all lovey-dovey, but he's not always that bad," I say. "We fight *and* we get along. Isn't that how all siblings are?"

Abbey and Darby look confused. "I don't know," Abbey says. "I was an only child before Mom got married."

"Me too," Darby says. There's a long pause, like they're both thinking. Then Darby asks, "Can I hold Spot's leash?"

"Of course!" I say. "We better get going. We have to find out where Spot and Swish came from before the animal shelter reopens!"

6

Biscuits and Baths

Pizza My Heart is a small and cozy shop. There are red-and-white tablecloths on all the tables, and the whole space smells like dough and tomato sauce. I remind myself to tell Dad later that we should come eat here sometime, instead of just getting delivery.

Then I look down at my shoes. *Uh-oh.* Last night, the pizza delivery person told us to wear rain boots, but I only have on my regular sneakers. I should have listened to him—the floor is as soggy as the tres leches cake I tried to make one time. You're supposed to pour milk over the top of the cake to make it moist and delicious. I figured adding twice as much milk would make it even more moist and delicious, but I was wrong! My cake turned into a soggy mess. There's an inch of water covering the floor in Pizza My Heart, and I can feel it creeping into my socks and shoes.

"Hello, there," a woman's voice calls out. I look up to see the owner of Pizza My Heart. She's a short woman who looks almost as old as my granny. I can tell she's good at cooking because she's covered in flour, just like Dad. I also know she's good at cooking because I've eaten a lot of her pizzas. She's wearing green rain boots that reach up to her knees.

"Sorry, we're only open for takeout. As you can see, we have a bit of a soggy bottom problem—wait, is that Sausage and Pepperoni?"

She smiles wide when she sees Spot and Swish. Pepper and Swish look at the water suspiciously, but Spot splashes around happily and even takes a quick drink. The pizza shop owner steps away from a huge brick oven and sloshes through the water on the floor to greet us. She looks at me hopefully. "Are you all their owners? I never knew they had any family."

My heart sinks. If she didn't know their family, that means she probably doesn't know where they came from.

"We're not their family," I say. "But we're trying to find their home. Yesterday they wandered into my family's cat café, The Purrfect Cup."

"Oh, that's right, I know your parents. We go to town business gatherings together sometimes. You must be Kira, then. Your parents called ahead, letting me know you might stop by," she says. "I'm Marianne. And your little brother, what's his name? Ryan? He calls over here a lot trying to place orders with a toy credit card."

I groan. "Sounds like Ryan. Do you have any idea where Spot and Swish came from? We want to make sure they don't end up in the shelter."

"I'm sorry, girls, I really don't," Marianne says. "These two are wanderers, that's for sure. They come by almost every day, looking happy as ever. I always give them a few snacks and some water. We call them Pepperoni and Sausage, but anchovies are their favorite."

"What's an anchovy?" Abbey asks. "A type of spider?"

"Abbey, shhh!" Darby says. "Anchovies are a type of fish."

"How was I supposed to know?" Abbey shrugs while Darby rolls her eyes.

"Please, Ms. Marianne," I say. "Do you have *any* clues about where they came from?"

"Hmm, I know they always come from that direction." She points out the window to the other side of the main street. "And you know, sometimes their fur is a little wet. And they smell like lavender. I'm not sure what that's about."

Lavender? Wet fur? Those sound like clues, but I have no idea what we're supposed to do now. Marianne gives Pepper, Spot, and Swish some anchovies while we think.

"Why would their fur be wet?" Abbey asks. "Do you think they went swimming somewhere?"

"Well . . . Dr. Delgado did say it seemed like

they got baths. Maybe they went swimming in a really clean puddle somewhere."

"Or maybe they got wet from the soggy floors," Darby says.

"No, that's not how they got wet," Marianne says. "Our leaky pipe is a new problem. I don't know what we're going to do."

She shakes her anchovy-filled fist in the direction of a big pipe along the back wall. Water falls from it, drip by drip, and plops onto the floor. I can't believe that those little drips add up to create all this mess. It makes me think about my other *great idea*. If I can find enough people who need Mrs. Talbot's help, it might be like those drips and add up to so much of her time that she can't ever come to tear down The Purrfect Cup. I take one of the business cards out of my pocket.

"I know someone who can help you with your soggy bottom problem!" I say. "Mrs. Talbot is new in town. She's available *right away* for urgent problems."

"Wow, thank you so much," Marianne says. "I didn't know we had a new contractor in town. I'm going to call her right now!"

Marianne runs to the back to call Mrs. Talbot, who says that she can come repair the pipe *in a few hours*! Marianne gives us a free pizza as a thank-you. Knowing that Mrs. Talbot is going to be busy is enough of a thank-you for me, but I don't say no to the pizza, either. Darby, Abbey,

and I ignore the water in our socks and sit down to take a few bites.

I hold a piece of pizza up to my nose and breathe deeply. It smells different than the pizza we had last night. I scrunch up my nose. "Do you smell that?" I ask. "That doesn't smell like perfectly greasy cheese."

Pepper, Spot, and Swish wiggle their noses and wag their tails. They seem to think the pizza smells *great*!

Abbey leans forward and smells Darby's hair. "Hold on a second. Darby, YOU smell like lavender! That's what Marianne said that Spot and Swish smelled like!"

Darby sniffs Abbey's hair. "You smell like lavender too!"

The girls smile like they both just got in on a super special secret. They turn to me together and say at the same time, "We know where Spot and Swish came from!"

❤🐾❤

"We just got our hair cut here this morning," Darby says. "Mrs. Thomas always uses lavender-scented shampoo."

We push the cat stroller into a hair salon called So Fresh and So Clean. It's a huge space with bright purple walls and lots of mirrors. Spot plops down onto the floor as soon as he gets inside.

"This place is so big, isn't it?" Darby says. "It's like our new house. At least this place is full of people. Our new house is big, but there's nothing to do. I don't even have anyone to climb the tree in the backyard with."

"What about Abbey?" I ask.

Abbey crosses her arms. "I don't want to bother the bugs that live in the tree."

Abbey and Darby are a lot like me and Ryan. Just a minute ago, they were solving a clue together! Now they're making faces at each other again.

"So you two had to move into a new house together?" I ask. I think about what Dad said about how he didn't like moving a lot as a kid. I bet Abbey and Darby don't like it, either.

"Yep," they say at the same time.

"My old house was so cute and cozy." Abbey sighs. "Like a cottage from a fairy tale. It had insects in every corner!"

"My old house was perfect," Darby says. "It was

right across the street from a playground, and Dad and I used to plant pink flowers in the garden. I wish we could go back."

As she talks, she reaches down and lays her hand on Swish's head. Swish nuzzles into her and purrs.

"I'm sorry," I say. "I know it's not the same, but my home is changing too. Mama and Dad want to tear down one of the walls in The Purrfect Cup. It's my favorite wall. I drew my first picture of Pepper and me there."

"Oh no," Abbey and Darby say together. "That's horrible."

"You know how they say you should never disturb a sleeping spider?" Abbey asks.

"No," I say.

"Well, lots of people say it. And I thi
should never disturb someone's home, either.

"Especially when the home was already perfect!" Darby agrees.

They both put their arms around me. I wish our parents understood why it's so hard to change homes. Maybe they should read more books about sleeping spiders.

Just then, Mrs. Thomas, the salon owner, sees us. She'd been busy blow-drying a customer's hair, but now she walks toward the front of the shop. Spot's tail starts wagging superfast when he sees her, and Swish stands on her back two legs to reach out for her.

"Hi, girls," Mrs. Thomas says as she picks Swish up. "Your hair is looking great. What are my two favorite human customers doing with my two favorite furry friends?"

"We're looking for their family!" Darby says. "Do they live with you?"

"No, I'm sorry," Mrs. Thomas says, shaking her head. "I don't know who their family is. All I know is that they wander in here almost every day, stinky and covered in biscuit crumbs. So I give them a nice warm bath, and some treats and water."

"Do you have any idea where they come from?" Abbey asks.

"They come wandering down the street

from that direction," Mrs. Thomas says. She points to the part of the main street that leads to the edge of town. "I see them a lot over by the salon's old location."

"The salon's old location?" I ask.

"We used to be in a spot down the road. We moved into this building because they have more space and better electricity. Hair dryers use a *lot* of energy!"

Pepper opens her mouth slowly. She looks like she can't believe what Mrs. Thomas is saying.

"You packed up your whole salon and moved?" I ask. I know I'm saying exactly what Pepper is thinking. "Don't you miss your old building?"

Mrs. Thomas looks thoughtful. "You know, I'll

always love that old building. I was so proud when I first started my business. But it was time to move on. I love this space too."

I raise an eyebrow at her, but then I remember my *great idea*. I clear my throat. "Well, I bet the new place could still use a little help to make it even better! Are you interested in hiring a contractor to do any work?"

"I have been thinking of finding someone to fix a few of the sinks in the back," Mrs. Thomas says. "But you girls are a little young for that kind of work, aren't you?"

"Yes, but we know the perfect person to help! And she's available *right away*. It sounds like those sinks really need to be fixed."

I hand her a business card. Mrs. Thomas offers to give Pepper a bath as a thank-you, but at the word *bath*, Pepper curls her back and all her hairs stand up straight. She shows Mrs. Thomas her teeth.

"Maybe that's not such a good idea," I say. "But thanks for your help! I'll come get a haircut after your sinks get fixed—hopefully REALLY soon!"

Abbey narrows her eyes at me as we leave the salon.

"What was that about? Seems like you have a spider up your sleeve."

"What—aaah!" I shake my arm around, trying to get rid of whatever creature is crawling around in my shirt. My movements scare Pepper, who jumps out of the stroller—and lands on Spot's head! He looks perfectly happy to have a cat-shaped hat. His tail wags so hard his whole body shakes and he accidentally knocks Pepper off his head.

"Relax, you don't have a spider on you," Darby says. "Abbey only meant that it seems like you're keeping a secret. And for the first time, I agree with her! Why do you keep handing out business cards?"

I tell them about my idea to keep Mrs. Talbot so busy that she won't ever have time to come back to The Purrfect Cup.

"Wow, Kira, you're as smart as a honeybee!" Abbey says. "If you didn't know, honeybees are the smartest insect in the world."

"Uh, thank you?" I say.

"I wish we had your idea when our parents were buying the new house," Darby says. "Maybe we could have stopped them from moving us in!"

Darby and Abbey agree to help me find more work for Mrs. Talbot. We keep following the clues to find out where Spot and Swish came from. No wonder Dr. Delgado said that they were healthy and well fed. They sure get a lot of love from the shops on the main road! Mrs. Thomas's clues lead us to the cookie shop where they get all their biscuits, and the biscuit man tells us he's seen Spot and Swish walking on the treadmill at the gym. That's probably how they get so stinky that they need one of Mrs. Thomas's lavender baths. The gym owner tells us that sometimes Spot and Swish have pet toys in their mouths when they show up to work out. That leads us to our town's pet shop where we get all the cat toys that we use at the café.

And everyone we visit says they could use help from Mrs. Talbot! The biscuit man wants help painting a new sign for his shop, and the gym owner needs to fix a hole in the wall made by someone who lifted too many weights. The pet shop owner's lights went out, and she needs help getting them to work again. I sure hope Mrs. Talbot helps her first—Pepper got really scared when the stroller rolled over a squeaky toy in the dark!

The pet shop owner says she doesn't know where Spot and Swish's home is. She tells us to try the last shop on the main road in town, Something Fishy. It's a fish shop owned by my friend Ellie and her family. Ellie and I became friends when she adopted a kitten from The Purrfect Cup. Now her kitten is best friends with a whole bunch of fish, which is funny because Pepper *eats* a whole bunch of fish in her cat food!

Behind the fish store, the town strip ends and there's some woods. No one lives back there. I start to get a little worried. If Ellie's mom doesn't know where Spot and Swish came from, what are we going to do?

We walk up to the door of Something Fishy, but before we go in, Spot looks at the woods excitedly and starts barking. I leave the stroller on the sidewalk and go over to pet him. Darby, Abbey, and I take turns scratching his belly until he calms down. But then, just as everything seems okay, I turn back to check on Pepper and Swish. *Oh no.* The mesh cover on the stroller isn't covering the cats anymore! We must have forgotten to put it back after we gave the cats treats at the cookie shop. Swish leaps out of the stroller and runs—straight into the woods.

7

Friends Fur-ever

"No, Swish!" I cry out. "Come back!"

It's too late. Swish disappears into the trees at the end of the main road in town. Spot pulls so hard on his leash that Darby has to run to keep up with him. At least Pepper doesn't jump out of the stroller. I hesitate. Mama said not to go off the main street, but I can't let Swish get away. And I don't think Mama would want me to let Darby run into the woods alone. I think she'd understand.

Abbey and I run into the woods after Darby and Spot. It's hard pushing the stroller over the bumpy ground and tree roots, but Abbey helps when I get stuck. By the time we catch up with Darby and Spot, I'm sweating!

"Over here!" Darby shouts. "I think I found out where Swish and Spot come from."

There's a hollowed-out tree trunk in front of her. Inside, Swish is curled up on an old blanket. I see treasures from all of Spot and Swish's adventures inside. There's a pizza crust, a brush from the salon, and some toys from the pet store. I realize that Spot and Swish really don't have a family, and my heart sinks. I feel so sad that they live out here in the woods alone. What will happen to them now?

Spot crawls into the trunk with Swish. But first, he spots a spider in the corner! He lifts it gently in his mouth so he doesn't squish it when he lies down. It climbs out of his mouth and settles on his nose. Spot doesn't mind. He turns around three times, then cuddles next to Swish in the tree trunk.

"Aww!" Abbey shouts. "He loves spiders!"

The three of them look so sweet that I can feel all three of my hearts swelling like a donut that's getting filled with jelly. We sit with Spot and Swish for a few minutes in the woods. But then Pepper meows loudly, and I remember that she's not an outdoor cat. We better get back to the main road and The Purrfect Cup.

We set Swish back into the stroller next to Pepper and head back to the café. The whole walk home, I think about what I'm going to say to Mama and Dad. There's no way they can separate Spot and Swish! They've been through so much together. Maybe I could promise to teach Spot how to use the litter box. Or I could say that if Spot goes to the animal shelter, Swish and I are going too! There's no reason to stay at The Purrfect Cup if it's all going to change, anyway.

In front of me, Darby and Abbey are walking with their heads together, whispering. I don't know what they're talking about, but they sure look like sisters!

Inside the café, Mr. and Mrs. Jacobson are sitting at a table playing with the tabby cats.

Mama and Dad look up from behind the counter when they see me walk in.

"How'd it go?" Dad asks. "We just got the call that the animal shelter is back open, so . . ."

Mama and Dad look at me hopefully. I can tell they don't want Spot to go, either.

"Well, we found out that Spot and Swish have lots of friends who take care of them. But they don't have a human family. They only have each other. And that's why—"

Darby interrupts me before I can finish talking.

"That's why Abbey and I want to bring them home!" she says. I gasp. Spot's ears perk up, and Swish's tail swishes happily. "Our new house has lots of room for a cat and a dog. And we have a big tree in the backyard, so they'll feel right at home because they're used to living in the woods. It's perfect."

"Plus, we can take them on walks to see all their old friends," Abbey says.

Mr. and Mrs. Jacobson look at each other, surprised. Mrs. Jacobson clears her throat. "Well, girls, we were really hoping that you might adopt sister cats. To help with, you know—"

"You don't have to be from the same litter to be family," says Darby. "Spot and Swish are proof of that. And so are we."

"Plus, Spot really loves bugs," Abbey says. "So we have to keep him."

They put their arms around each other and look at their parents.

"Oh dear," says Mr. Jacobson. "Our kids are smarter than us."

I smile. I think that means Spot and Swish just found a home. They've been *best friends fur-ever* for a long time, but now they get to be something even better.

Family.

I think about how I felt when I saw them in the tree trunk. I was sad that they were all alone out there. But now I realize that they were never alone—they had each other! Maybe a home isn't always a place, like The Purrfect Cup or Darby's and Abbey's old houses. Maybe home is more about who lives inside.

Dad said that home is more than paint and walls. Maybe for Spot and Swish, home is more than a blanket in the woods. It's wherever they can be together, and it's all the people all over town who care for them. And now, it's Abbey and Darby and the Jacobsons.

Abbey and Darby finally look happy about their new house. They're whispering about all the things they can do to make it feel like more of a home for Spot and Swish. And everyone in town was excited to get Mrs. Talbot's help to make their shops feel more like home too. If they can change, maybe I can too.

The Purrfect Cup isn't home because of the colors on the walls or the wobbly shelves. It's home because it's filled with everyone I love—Mama, Dad, all the cats, and even Ryan. The Purrfect Cup may change and grow, just like my *great ideas*, but it'll always be home. It'll always be perfect.

I look at the wall that Mrs. Talbot is going to move and notice that there's already a hole cut out in it. My chest feels tight, but I take a deep breath and turn to Mama.

"Did Mrs. Talbot already start working on The Purrfect Cup?" I ask.

Mama chuckles. "No, Mrs. Talbot is a bit too busy for that. It was nice of you to get her so much new business."

I gulp, but Mama doesn't look upset.

"Kira, Mrs. Talbot wasn't going to start work on the café today. We need time to get ready to move the cats! We're going to do it when your school has winter vacation."

"But Mrs. Talbot said she was going to

come back to The Purrfect Cup today."

"Only because I told her that we were going to start selling avocado toast, and she wanted to try some." Mama clears her throat. "I mean, avo-*cat*-o toast. That was a good idea, Kira."

I smile. "And it will be nice to have a little more space in the café. Who knew your *great ideas* could be as good as mine, Mama!"

We laugh together.

"But wait, if Mrs. Talbot was only here for toast, why is there a hole in the wall?" I ask.

"I'll let your dad explain," Mama says. She smiles as Dad walks out from the kitchen. He has something big and bulky sticking out from behind his back.

"All right, Kira, close your eyes," Dad says.

I squeeze them shut, and he places something big and square shaped in my hands. "What is this? A Pizza My Heart box?"

"Good guess." Dad chuckles. "You can open your eyes."

I open them and start smiling right away. It's the piece of the wall with my crayon drawing of Pepper and me.

"We thought you could hang it in your room," Dad says. "So you'll always remember The Purrfect Cup exactly how it was when you first stepped inside."

"Thanks, Dad," I say. "I love it. And I can't wait to meet The Purrfect Cup 2.0. Actually, I have a few ideas for Mrs. Talbot. When's she coming by?"

"All right, all right," Mama says. "I think you've given Mrs. Talbot enough work for one day."

"Tomorrow, then," I say.

I look at my family. My *home*. Mama and Dad smile at me proudly, and Ryan looks up from his iPad to wink at me. Pepper jumps out of the stroller and into my arms. Her whiskers tickle my chin, and I wonder if my family is like that hair on my chin that reaches into my brain and helps me think of *great ideas*. With them around, I know I'm going to have more ideas.

A *lot* more.

Read about all of
Kira's GREAT ideas!

Home
for Meow
The Purrfect Show
Reese Eschmann
SCHOLASTIC

Home
for Meow
Show and Tail
Reese Eschmann
SCHOLASTIC

Home
for Meow
Kitten
Around
Reese Eschmann
SCHOLASTIC

Home
for Meow
Two Fur One
Reese Eschmann
SCHOLASTIC

Read on for a sneak peak at the

latest adventure at

THE PUPPY PLACE

Chapter One

"Over here, Buddy!" Lizzie clapped her hands and watched, smiling, as her little brown puppy looked up, spotted her, and dashed toward her, leaving behind a cluster of other dogs in all different sizes and shapes.

"What a good boy," Lizzie said as Buddy sat panting in front of her. She popped a liver treat into his mouth and he gobbled it down, wagging his tail. Then he grinned up at her and wagged his tail even harder. You didn't have to be able to speak Dog to know what he was saying.

"You want more treats?" Lizzie asked. She laughed. "Maybe later. Go on and play." She waved him away, and Buddy zipped off to meet up with another bunch of dogs, over by the wading pool. Lizzie shook her head as she watched him go. Buddy really was such a good dog. Even here at the dog park, with so many wonderful distractions, he came to her when she called.

Lizzie loved the dog park almost as much as Buddy did. She loved watching all the different dogs play together. There were big ones and small ones, shy dogs and outgoing pups—and they all seemed to get along. Their owners were interesting, too. There were young couples, older people, and sometimes a mom or dad who was juggling kids and dogs, running from the playground to the dog park and back again.

Why didn't she come more often? Lizzie usually only went to the dog park when she had a foster puppy who needed some extra socialization—that is, a puppy who needed to learn how to get along with other dogs and people.

Lizzie's family, the Petersons, were a foster family for puppies who needed homes. They took each one in just for a little while, until they could find the perfect home for that puppy. Every puppy was different, and Lizzie loved getting to know them and figuring out what type of home would be best.

With most puppies, it was enough to stay home and play with Buddy in the Petersons' fenced yard. Buddy had started out as a foster puppy, but he'd ended up being a permanent part of the family. Now, along with Lizzie's younger brothers, Charles and the Bean, Buddy helped each new foster puppy feel at home. He was always friendly and welcoming, always ready to share his toys, his treats, and his family.

But it had been a little while since their last foster puppy, and Lizzie had started to wonder if Buddy was feeling a bit bored and lonely. The dog park was the perfect solution. He could run and play and meet new dogs—without even having to share his toys!

Now Buddy was zooming around in circles, chasing and being chased—two of his favorite things to do. In front of Buddy was a tiny, fluffy, rust-colored Pomeranian, yapping his head off as he scampered along. Behind Buddy was a big, galumphing golden retriever who wagged her feathery tail as she ran, letting out deep woof-woofs, as if yelling, "Wait for me, wait for me!"

Soon, some other dogs joined the fun: Lizzie spotted a sleek gray Weimaraner and a curly-haired Airedale mix. (Lizzie could identify the breed of pretty much any dog she saw, since she was always studying the Dog Breeds of the World poster on her bedroom wall.) Then she saw a pair of brown-and-white spaniels that looked very familiar. "Zig! Zag!" Lizzie yelled when she saw them. They had been two of her favorite foster pups, even if they had been quite a handful. The hardest part had been telling them apart since they were practically twins. Their coloring was exactly the same, with each brown spot in the same place on each pup. Lizzie headed over to talk to their owner. She didn't always get a chance to see her foster puppies once they were adopted. She couldn't wait to hear how they were doing.

"Hey, Lizzie!"

Lizzie turned—and groaned. Her best friend, Maria, was running toward her across the dog park.

Lizzie loved Maria, she really did. But she knew why Maria was here.

"Your mom told me you were here. I thought we were going to get together after dog-walking, to talk about the sleepover!" Maria said breathlessly as she approached.

Lizzie, Maria, and two other friends had a dog-walking business. Every day after school, they walked dogs for people who needed a little help with their pets. Lizzie usually did some training as well, since she loved helping dogs learn how to be their best selves. She was always happy to help when a client begged her to teach a dog to stop barking, or come when called.

She and Maria had both done their dog-walking

routes that day, but then Lizzie had "forgotten" that they'd made plans to meet. "Oh, right," she said now. "Sure." Maria was really excited about a sleepover party she was planning, and Lizzie—wasn't. Why? Because it was going to be a Spooky Sleepover, where everyone told their scariest stories.

Scary stories were very popular lately in Lizzie's grade. Everyone talked about the horror movies they'd watched over the weekend, or the Goosebumps books they were reading.

Lizzie didn't watch horror movies.

She didn't read scary stories.

She did not see the point. Wasn't being scared a bad thing? It was for her. If she heard a scary story it stuck with her forever, keeping her awake at night. Why did people think it was fun to be scared? She just didn't get it—but so far, she had not shared these feelings with Maria. She didn't want her best friend to think she was a chicken, or a baby.

"Yeah, great!" Lizzie pasted on a big smile, pretending to be excited about the party. "I'm so glad you found me. So tell me what you're thinking."

Maria started to talk about skeleton decorations—"Like a family of skeletons, maybe even a dog skeleton, maybe the kind that move!" she said—and about scary snacks, like hot dogs made to look like bloody fingers.

Lizzie nodded and smiled. She didn't even